SMALL ONE'S ADVENTURE

DEDICATION

For my husband,
for whom I daily give thanks. –D.M.

To, Ollie, my loving and supportive
(in spite of my long hours) husband. –P.F.

All About Kids Publishing
6280 San Ignacio Ave., Ste. D
San Jose, CA 95119

Editor: Lisa M. Tooker
Book Design: Alice Merrill

Manufactured in China

Library of Congress Cataloging-in-Publication Data

Mueller, Doris.
Small One's Adventure / by Doris Mueller ; illustrated by Parker Fulton.
p.   cm.
Summary: When her eagerness to be one of the big elephants gets her in trouble at
the watering hole, Small One discovers some nice things about still being young.
ISBN 0-9710278-1-1 (hardcover)
[1. Elephants—Fiction. 2. Size—Fiction.] I. Fulton, Parker, ill. II. Title.
PZ7.M8786 Sm   2002
[E]—dc21
2001007463

SMALL ONE'S ADVENTURE

BY DORIS L. MUELLER

ILLUSTRATED BY PARKER FULTON

all about kids
publishing

The African sun blazed fiercely in the afternoon sky, and Small One was hot and thirsty. The young elephant peeked through her mother's knees hoping to see the river waterhole. But a forest of legs, like tall gray posts, blocked her view. Her family surrounded her, protecting her from lions and other predators. They think I'm a toto—a baby—she thought, as they plodded toward the water.

Small One followed her mother, stumbling now and then over a large clump of grass or a rock. She could hardly wait to reach the river. Like all elephants, she loved the water, not only to quench her thirst and cool her off, but also to play in.

"Are we almost there?" asked Small One.
"Just a little longer," her mother rumbled back, stroking the calf with her trunk.

Small One thought greedily of how she would drink all the cool water and roll in the soft, dark mud. "I hope there'll be other calves there to play with," said Small One, as her feet danced with impatience.

"There will be," promised her mother.

Today, I'm going to use my trunk for drinking like the older ones, Small One reassured herself. So far all I've done is blow bubbles!

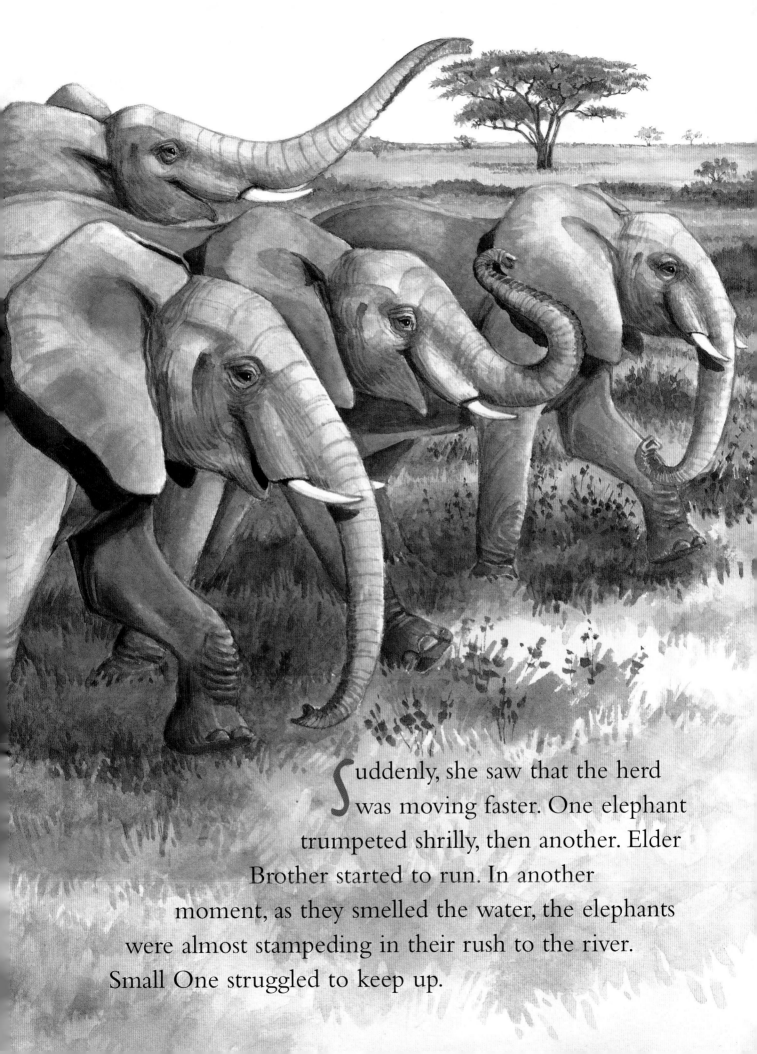

Suddenly, she saw that the herd was moving faster. One elephant trumpeted shrilly, then another. Elder Brother started to run. In another moment, as they smelled the water, the elephants were almost stampeding in their rush to the river. Small One struggled to keep up.

Big Mama, the matriarch got there first and waded in the shallow water. The rest of the herd lumbered behind, trumpeting loudly. They milled around, greeting

friends and relatives from other family groups. They
sucked water through their trunks to squirt down their
throats and to spray themselves and each other.

Another cow elephant that was proudly showing her twins greeted Small One's mother. They were very handsome, but Small One could hardly wait to begin playing. She moved carefully away from the older elephants, blowing bubbles as she went. Sometimes she managed to suck up enough water with her trunk to squirt a few drops down her throat.

She climbed on her big sister who was lying in a shallow
mudhole. When her sister rolled over, Small One slipped,
splashing into the water and its soft brown bottom.

Small One giggled. "This is fun!" She rolled from side to
side, covering herself with a layer of cool, thick mud. She
could see her aunties glance her way as she drifted slightly
away from the herd. Her mother rumbled a warning to be
careful. Small One pretended not to hear.

"I'm big! I don't have to stay close to my mother all the time," she trumpeted, to no one in particular.

Slowly the elephants began to go ashore. They climbed out, dripping mud and water, and the bank became even steeper and more slippery.

Small One noticed that the twins needed help. They wrapped their trunks around their aunties' tails, pulling themselves safely to shore. Small One smiled. "I can climb out by myself."

Small One's mother must have heard her. "Come out, Small One," she called. The calf tossed her head.

"In a minute." Proudly, she sucked up water to squirt down her throat. "I'm big!" she repeated.

Her mother called again and swung her front foot. Small One knew what that meant—her mother was about to come after her. It was time to obey.

Small One started up the steep
bank, but she lost her footing and
slid back into the muddy river. Hoping no
one had noticed, she tried again. This time she
made it almost halfway before sliding back. She
pulled her front feet out of the mud and took a step.
But now her back feet were stuck, and she fell back.
Again and again she tried to climb the bank, but each
time she slipped back. Small One was scared. "Help!"
she squealed.

Her mother hurried toward her, rumbling orders loudly. At once, two aunties got behind Small One and pushed. Her mother reached out her trunk and Small One clutched it tightly with her own. With a loud slushing sound, her feet finally came loose, and the calf found herself in a heap on the shore.

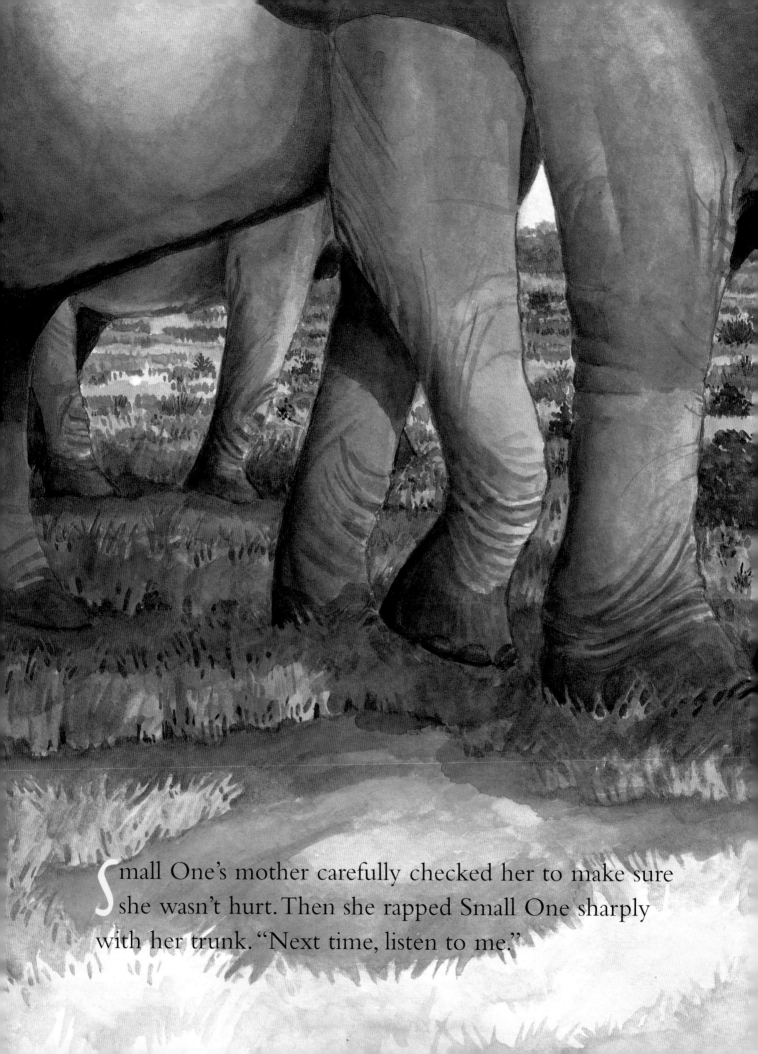

Small One's mother carefully checked her to make sure she wasn't hurt. Then she rapped Small One sharply with her trunk. "Next time, listen to me."

Tearfully, Small One scooted to her safe place among the
tall gray legs. The herd plodded away from the waterhole
to feed and to rest. Small One said, "I'm sorry I didn't
obey you, Mother. I guess I'm not quite ready to be big."

Her mother stroked her gently. When the herd paused, Small One peered up at her mother. "I didn't just blow bubbles today. I sucked water with my trunk like you do."

Her mother patted her and said, "I know. You're growing up."

Reaching up with her tiny trunk, Small One took a bite of juicy grass from her mother's mouth. Someday she would be big. But for now she was glad just to be Small One, with her family all around her.